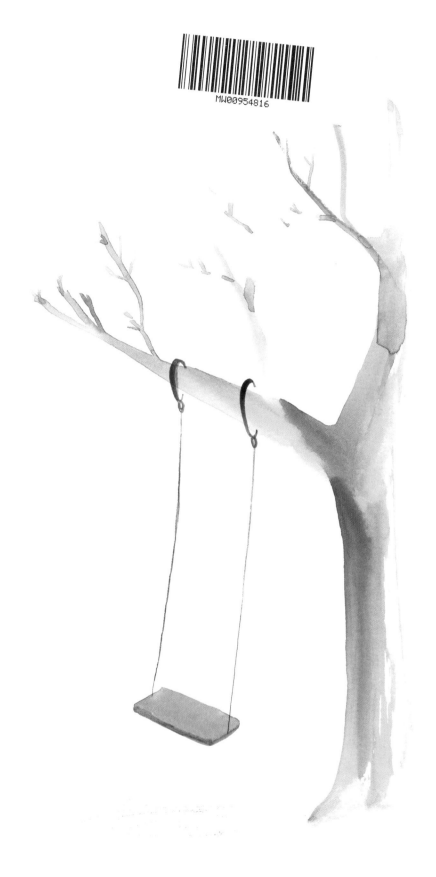

25 24 23 22 21 20 19   1 2 3 4 5 6 7 8

ISBN: 978-1-5064-4872-5

Library of Congress Cataloging-in-Publication Data

Names: Webb, Amy, 1977- author. | Liddiard, Merrilee, illustrator.
Title: When Charley met Emma / written by Amy Webb ; illustrated by Merrilee
    Liddiard.
Description: First edition. | Minneapolis, MN : Beaming Books, 2019. |
    Summary: Five-year-old Charley gets teased for daydreaming and drawing
    more than his friends, but when he meets Emma, who is physically
    different, he needs help remembering that being different is okay.
Identifiers: LCCN 2018030769 | ISBN 9781506448725 (hard cover : alk. paper)
Subjects: | CYAC: Individuality--Fiction. | Friendship--Fiction. | People
    with disabilities--Fiction.
Classification: LCC PZ7.1.W4178 Whe 2019 | DDC [E]--dc23 LC record available at https://lccn.loc.gov/2018030769

VN0004589;9781506448725;JAN2019

Beaming Books
510 Marquette Avenue
Minneapolis, MN 55402
Beamingbooks.com≠≠

When CHARLEY *met* EMMA

written by Amy Webb   illustrated by Merrilee Liddiard

beaming books
MINNEAPOLIS

Charley liked to do lots of different things.

Sometimes Charley liked to be loud and wild. He liked to climb and swing and run with his friends.

But Charley also liked to be quiet. He liked to sit and think and draw by himself. This made Charley feel different.

But whenever Charley felt different, he remembered what his mother taught him.

Different isn't weird,
    sad, bad, or strange.
  Different is different. And different
              is OK!

One day, Charley and his mother went to the park, and he saw someone even more different than he was.

Charley stopped and stared. He saw a girl without any hands! And she was in a wheelchair! He rubbed his eyes and looked again . . . Yep! Still no hands!

What happened? Where did her hands go?

Maybe some aliens came from outer space and took her hands with them!

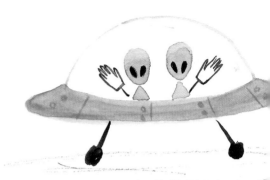

Or maybe a monster had bitten them off!

BURP!

Or maybe her hands were just lost!

looking for LOST HANDS

Charley had a strange feeling inside his stomach. Before he knew what was happening, he heard himself asking in a not-so-quiet voice,

Charley looked up and noticed that his mom's face looked weird too. Charley looked at the girl and saw that she looked sad. Now Charley's stomach started to *hurt*.

Charley's mom knelt down next to Charley. "Sweetie, it's not nice to call people weird. Weird is a rude word. Rude words can hurt people's feelings. She's not weird. She's different. Do you remember what I taught you about being different?"

Charley remembered.

But *was* different OK? Maybe this girl was *too* different. Maybe this girl *was* strange.

"You should introduce yourself," Charley's mom said. "I bet she likes making new friends too."

"Hi. I'm Charley. What's your name?"

"I'm Emma," the girl said.

"And this is my sister Chloe."

"I'm sorry I said you look weird," said Charley. "My mommy says that's a me[an] word."

"That's right," Emma said. "I also don't like it when people point, stare, laugh or whisper about me."

"But it's okay if you have questions," Emma said.

Charley smiled. He did have questions—lots of them.
"Why don't you have any hands?" he asked. "And why do
you have that chair?"

Emma sat up straight and smiled. "I was born this way. I have limb differences. That means my arms and legs are different. I can't walk, so I use this wheelchair. I drive it all by myself."

"Wow," Charley said. "You really *are* different."

"Yep," said Emma. "I am. Lots of people are different!"

"Some people can't hear or speak and need to use their hands to communicate."

"Some people need special machines to help them walk or breathe."

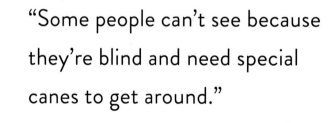

"Some people can't see because they're blind and need special canes to get around."

"All of us are different sizes, shapes, and colors! We're all different in one way or another. Do you ever feel different, Charley?"

Charley thought for a second and then told them about how he sometimes liked to run and play and shout like his friends—and sometimes liked to sit and think and draw.

"Yeah," said Chloe, "Some people are different on the inside and some people are different on the outside. But we're all different!"

"We're all different," Charlie repeated. "And different is okay!"

"That's right!" Emma said. "I am a little *differenter* than you, but I'm a lot the same too!"

"You are?" asked Charley. "How?"

"I like to play on the playground," said Emma.

"Me too!" said Charley.

"I like to swing!" said Emma.

"Me too!" said Charley.

"I even like to play tag with my friends."

"Wow," said Charley. "Me *too!*"

Then Charley said, "My favorite thing in the whole world is drawing. I really like to draw."

With a big smile on her face, Emma grabbed a pencil with her foot and wrote something on Charley's notebook.

Soon it was time for Charley and his mom to go home. "Good-bye, Emma! Good-bye, Chloe! Let's play again soon!"

Emma and Chloe yelled back, "Good-bye, Charley!"

As Charley and his mom walked home, Charley said, "Mom, I made a new friend today. My friend Emma is different than me, but different isn't weird, ad, bad, or strange! Different is just different, and guess what? I think ifferent is GREAT!"

For Parents and Caregivers

When meeting a child or person with special needs it's important to educate your children about differences and to foster friendships with kids of all different abilities. Remember this 4-step plan.

1 **Educate or teach.** Don't shush your child and walk away. Instead, tell your child that it's okay if they have questions. Ask the child with special needs what their name is. Ask the child or caregiver about their differences.

2 **Reinforce kindness.** Teach your child that while questions are okay, staring, pointing whispering, and laughing are not. Help your child learn to use kind words like "different" instead of hurtful words like "weird," "creepy," or "ugly."

3 **Find common ground.** Help your child understand that we are more alike than different. Find commonalities they both have—favorite toys, food, games, activities, and/or movies are some great starting points.

4 **Emphasize different abilities.** Every person is good at something. Help your child learn that while a person with disabilities might not be able to do certain things, they are probably good at lots of other things. They may even have some abilities that you don't have!

Amy Webb is an artist, writer, mother, and creator of the popular blog This Little Miggy Stayed Home. As a special needs mom she advocates for the disability and special needs community through her writings and interviews on her blog. Her work has been featured in The Mighty, A Cup of Jo, and Design*Sponge as well as interviews in DesignMom, MotherMag, and the print publication Lunch Lady Magazine. Amy lives with her husband and three beautiful daughters in Cincinnati, Ohio.